Princess
Yellow Boots
Finds a Friend

Lynn H. and Dani Elliott

STANSBURY
PUBLISHING
Chico, Ca.

Princess Yellow Boots Finds a Friend
Copyright © 2019 by Lynn H. Elliott
and Dani Elliott

First Edition
Printed in the United States of America
Illustrations by Steve Ferchaud of Chico

ISBN: 978-1-935807-48-3
Library of Congress Control Number: 2019954174

Stansbury Publishing
An Imprint of Heidelberg Graphics
2 Stansbury Court
Chico, California 95928

For Grace

(the inspiration for our story)
With Love
Granddad and Granny Dani

Princess Froth woke up angry. She'd gone to bed angry and spent a restful night, tossing and turning—and angry.

She jumped out of bed and stormed across to her large shoe closet. They weren't there. Hundreds and hundreds of shoes, but not the ones she wanted.

"Good morning, princess," said her maid entering.

"It is not a good morning," Princess Froth growled. "Where is the kitchen? Take me there!"

"The kitchen?" the maid asked.

"Are you deaf?" snapped Princess Froth. "I said, Take me to the kitchen, stupid woman."

"But, but ... "

"Stop stammering and take me there."

The maid was shocked. Six-year-old Princess Froth had never been to the palace kitchen. Why should she go there? That was where the servants cooked food and prepared for the large banquets. It was not a place for a princess.

Princess Froth stamped her feet and went red in the face. "Take me there! Now!"

And so the maid took Princess Froth downstairs to the kitchen. The kitchen staff quickly bowed up at the sight of the princess. "Where is the girl?" yelled Princess Froth.

A small girl peeked from behind the cook's apron. She raised her hand. "Yes, you," growled Princess Froth. "Come here!" The girl walked slowly forward. "What is your name?"

"Grace," whispered the girl.

"Speak up!" shouted the princess.

"Grace, your majesty."

Princess Froth looked down at

Grace's feet. "Why are you barefoot?"

"I have no shoes, your majesty."

"You're lying," Princess Froth yelled. "I watched you walking home through the snow last night. You were wearing squeaky yellow rubber boots."

"I only wear those in the snow, your majesty."

"Bring them to me. Now!"

The girl hurried to the back room where all the cloaks and shoes were kept. She picked up her squeaky yellow boots and took them to the princess.

"Give them to me!" said the princess. "They are mine now."

"But what will I have to walk home in the snow, your majesty?"

"Why are you asking me?" growled the princess. "Someone else can give you shoes, or you can go barefoot." The princess took off her shoes and replaced them with the yellow boots. "From now on, I shall be called Princess Squeaky Yellow Boots. Understand?"

"Yes, Princess Squeaky Yellow Boots," the kitchen staff replied.

The princess marched off proudly repeating, "Princess Squeaky Yellow Boots, Princess Squeaky Yellow Boots!"

The young girl, Grace, ran back

to the cook who held the young girl.
"We'll find something for you to wear
back through the snow."

*A*ll that day, Princess Froth stomped through the palace, demanding everyone, even the king and queen, call her Princess Squeaky Yellow Boots.

And Grace went home through the snow, wearing no shoes and three pairs of borrowed socks that were soon cold and wet.

*T*hat night, Princess Squeaky Yellow Boots went to bed, proudly placing her new yellow boots in the closet with her hundreds of other shoes.

At midnight, the princess was awakened by a thumping and squeaking sound. Thump, thump, thump. Squeak, squeak, squeak. She got out of bed, lit a candle, and walked around the room. She opened her bedroom door. Nothing. The thumping and squeaking had stopped, so she climbed back into bed.

Five minutes later: thump, thump,

thump, squeak, squeak, squeak. Again the princess got out of bed, lit a candle, and walked around the room. The thumping stopped.

A third time: thump, thump, thump, squeak, squeak, squeak. The princess sat up in bed, lit a candle and screamed, "Maid! Maid, where are you?"

The maid rushed into the room. "Something is going thump, thump, thump, squeak, squeak, squeak," the princess snarled. "Find it!"

The maid looked everywhere, but could not find the thump or the squeak. "Are you sure you looked everywhere?" growled the princess.

"Yes, ma'am," replied the frightened maid.

"I'll get back into bed and you can sleep on the floor for the rest of the night."

The princess got back into bed and pulled the covers back over herself. The maid blew out the candle and lay on the stone floor, shivering with cold.

Thump, thump, thump! Squeak, squeak, squeak!

The maid jumped up and lit the candle. "Find whatever it is and throw it out in the snow," snarled the princess.

The maid searched the room. The sound was coming from the closet filled with shoes. As soon as the door opened, the squeaky yellow boots walked out.

"The squeaky yellow boots were kicking the door, your majesty," said the maid. "And now they're leaving the room."

"That's impossible!" the princess snarled. "Boots don't walk by themselves. They have to be put on feet— my feet!"

"But look!" replied the maid.

The princess and the maid watched as the boots continued toward the staircase.

"Follow them!" the princess ordered.

Princess and maid hurried after the squeaky yellow boots. Soon other members of the staff joined the procession. "Stop!" yelled the princess, standing in front of the boots. The boots marched around her, one on each side. "Stop them!" she repeated. A servant boy jumped forward, grabbing ahold of the boots. On they marched, dragging the servant boy behind them as they headed to the outer door of the castle.

Thump, thump, thump! Squeak, squeak, squeak! The boots kicked at the outer door. "Don't open the door," yelled the princess. But the doors opened suddenly by themselves. No sooner had the boots exited the castle, than the doors closed behind them.

"Follow those boots!" screamed the princess. "Bring them back to me!"

But no matter how many of the staff pulled at the door, it would not open.

That night no one in the palace slept. The princess howled all night long. "Where are my squeaky yellow boots?"

As soon as it was light, Princess Froth

rushed to the window. Impossible! There was that ragged young girl, Grace, walking to the castle—in the squeaky yellow boots. "Thief! Thief!" the princess screamed, rushing down the stairs and into the kitchen. "Take those squeaky yellow boots from her. They're mine! Throw her in prison!"

The squeaky yellow boots were ripped from Grace's feet, handed to the princess, and Grace was marched downstairs to the prisons.

"Once again," Princess Froth declared. "I am Princess Squeaky Yellow Boots."

She put on the boots and tried marching to the throne room. But the boots suddenly changed direction, almost throwing the princess to the ground.

On they marched despite the princess' orders. They marched through the door leading downstairs to the prison and didn't stop until they stood before the prison. Grace sat, quietly

crying, on the stone floor of one of the cold, wet cells. Rats scuttled across the floor, and spiders hung their webs from the ceilings.

"Did you tell these boots to come

down here?" the princess demanded.

"No," Grace replied.

"Then why are they making me walk down here?"

"I don't know."

Princess Froth tried to turn around to march back to the throne room, but the boots wouldn't move. They stayed facing Grace.

"Have you put a spell on these boots?"

"No, princess."

"Where did you get them?"

"An old woman gave them to me."

"Where was this old woman?" the princess demanded.

"In the village market, your majesty."

"You will take me to this market and I shall get my own pair of squeaky yellow boots from this old woman. Let her out of prison!"

And so they went to the village market: Grace marching in her squeaky yellow boots, and the princess following in a horse-drawn carriage.

Soon they stood before the old woman's stall. The princess pointed at a pair of squeaky yellow rubber boots. "I want those," she demanded.

"But do those boots want you?" the old woman asked.

"What sort of silly question is that?"

"I ask it again: Do those boots want

you as a friend? Ask them!"

"That is ridiculous," the princess replied. "I have money and, if I want, I can simply take them and throw you in prison."

"Yes, you have money, and you can throw me in prison, but still you have not answered the question. Do the boots want you as a friend?"

The princess leapt out of her carriage and grabbed at the squeaky yellow boots. But pull as she might, the boots would not leave the table before the old woman's stall. "I demand you come to me," the princess snapped, talking to the boots.

Even the guard protecting the princess could not rip the boots from the table.

She was about to get back into her carriage when the old woman stopped her.

"Do you have any friends?" the old woman asked.

The princess pointed to Grace.

"She's my friend."

"No. She's a serving girl," replied the old woman. "Grace cleans your floors and washes your clothes. That's not friendship. Look around you."

The princess looked. The village children were dancing, giggling, chasing and playing games with each other.

The princess felt sad. She jumped into her carriage, slammed the door and was taken back to the castle.

That night, she woke up. Thump, thump, thump. Squeak, squeak, squeak. She jumped out of bed and threw open the closet door. Nothing. No squeaky yellow boots.

She slammed the door shut and stomped back to bed. Thump, thump, thump. Squeak, squeak, squeak.

"Maid!" she screamed.

The maid rushed in. "Stop that thumping and squeaking," the princess demanded.

"What thumping and squeaking? I hear nothing."

"There it is. From the closet."

The maid opened the closet door. Nothing.

"Can't you hear it?" screamed the princess. "Call the guards!"

More guards and maids came into

the princess' bedroom, but no one could hear the thumping or squeaking. No one except Princess Froth.

The princess didn't sleep all night.

Next morning the princess rushed down to the kitchen. She grabbed Grace. "Where are those boots?"

"In the back room, princess."

"Did you wear them home last night?"

"Yes."

"Then why did I hear them in my bedroom in the night?"

"I lay with them under my pillow all night. They didn't move, your majesty."

The princess was silent.

"Can I go now, your majesty? I have a lot of work to do before I go back to the village."

There was no answer. Grace looked at the princess. A tear slowly moved down Princes Froth's face.

"Are you crying, your majesty?" The princess turned away from

Grace. "No," the princess sniffed. "Yesterday, in the village, the children seemed so happy, even though they had nothing."

"They had each other, your majesty."

The princess dropped her head, trying to hold back a sob.

Grace took the princess' hand in hers. "You don't have anyone to laugh and play with, do you? You have no friends."

The princess shook her head.

"I don't know how to be a friend," the princess replied.

"It's not hard. As you laugh and play together, you learn things about the other person and want to help them. I can be your friend."

"But we're so different. I'm so ... and you're so ... "

"But we're both little girls. Do you like to laugh and play?"

"Princesses don't laugh or play."

"But little girls and boys do. I

laugh and play with my sister and brother."

"I don't have a sister or a brother."

"Maybe I can be your sister. You can laugh and play with me and my sister and brother."

"But wherever I go ..."

Grace ran to the princess' closet. She looked through the clothes. "No, no, no. Maybe this."

Grace held a plain dress in her hands.

"But those are the clothes I wear when I ride my horse," the princess said, "not when I visit people."

"But if you wear these, you'll look just like one of the girls of the village. And we can rub some dirt on your cheeks."

The princess giggled as she changed her clothes. "Let's go the village now."

"What about my chores?" Grace replied.

"I'll help you with them. I'll keep my head down, so nobody sees my face and knows who I am."

Grace and her helper worked hard cleaning the kitchen and washing the clothes and sheets. When it was time to leave, Grace put on her squeaky yellow boots and left, followed by Princess Froth.

The maid rushed through the palace. "Princess Froth has disappeared," she cried. "Where is the princess?" Guards and maids rushed up and down stairs, peering into every room and every closet to find the princess.

Meanwhile, in the village, a new girl was playing with her newfound sisters and brothers. They threw balls, played hopscotch and skimmed stones across the nearby lake. The princess squealed with delight when chased by the others. Until she ran into the arms of a palace guard. He stared into the flushed, dirty face. "Princess? Is that you?"

The guard turned to Grace, her
sister and brother. "You are in seri-
ous trouble," he yelled. "When the

queen and king hear of this, you'll be flogged and thrown into prison."

Princess Froth marched over to Grace and the other children and put her arms around them. "You will not touch any of these children," she said. "These are all my friends. Grace, her brother and sister will come to the palace every day, not to work but to laugh and play with me. They are my friends."

That night the princess was awakened as she slept in her bed. Thump, thump, thump. She ran across to the closet and flung open the door. A shiny pair of squeaky yellow boots marched across the room and jumped up into Princess Froth's bed. She crawled in beside them and smiled as she held them tight.

And she slept.

www.ingramcontent.com/pod-product-compliance
Lightning Source LLC
Chambersburg PA
CBHW050919120626
46552CB00004B/1666